"Now what am I going to do?"

Salem couldn't believe it. He was locked out of the house! He jumped back to the ground and breathed deeply to calm himself. Then he tried to convince himself that things could be worse.

There wasn't anything in his own front yard that could hurt him—

Grrrr!

Salem's eyes snapped wide open. *Was that my stomach?*

Something growled again.

The deep, throaty snarl made two very important facts perfectly clear to Salem.

It was a very *big* dog, and it was very, very *close.*

"I'm doomed!" Salem wailed.

Sabrina, the Teenage Witch™
Salem's Tails™

#1 CAT TV
    Salem Goes to Rome
#2 Teacher's Pet
#3 You're History!
#4 The King of Cats
#5 Dog Day Afternoon

Available from MINSTREL Books

Salem's Tails™

DOG DAY AFTERNOON

Diana G. Gallagher

Based on Characters Appearing in Archie Comics

**And based upon the television series
Sabrina, The Teenage Witch
Created for television by Nell Scovell
Developed for television by Jonathan Schmock**

Illustrated by Mark Dubowski

A
MINSTREL®
BOOK

Published by POCKET BOOKS
New York   London   Toronto   Sydney   Tokyo   Singapore

A MINSTREL PAPERBACK *Original*

 A Minstrel Book published by
POCKET BOOKS, a division of Simon & Schuster Inc.
1230 Avenue of the Americas, New York, NY 10020

Salem Quotes taken from the following episodes:
"Jenny's Non-Dream" written by Jon Sherman
"Mars Attracts" written by Nell Scovell

ISBN: 0-671-02103-6

First Minstrel Books printing March 1999

10 9 8 7 6 5 4 3 2 1

Printed in the U.S.A.   692429

For my grandson
Jonathan J. Streb,
the singer

Hey, the whole point of a family vacation is so I can get a vacation from the family.

—*Salem*

DOG DAY AFTERNOON

Chapter 1

"Why can't I go?" Salem whined as he followed Aunt Hilda down the stairs.

"Because you're a cat." Aunt Hilda stopped by the front door.

"Exactly! I'm a cat. And I never get to go anywhere!" Salem sat down on the bottom step. He crossed his front paws for luck. Then he hung his head

and sighed. His super-sad look almost always got him more tuna.

But it didn't get him anything this time.

"I'm not taking you to the Fresh Fish Market, Salem," Aunt Hilda said. "You'd sample every fish in sight. And then I'd have to buy them."

Salem sighed as visions of rainbow trout and silver cod swam through his head. If there was one thing in the whole world he loved more than anything, it was fresh fish. For breakfast, lunch, dinner, and midnight snacks.

"I'll be good!" Raising his right front paw, Salem begged. "Cat's honor."

Aunt Hilda started to leave, then paused.

Whiskers twitching, Salem perked up. Maybe she had changed her mind!

Nope.

Aunt Hilda snapped her fingers and a black purse magically appeared in her hand. "Can't go shopping the mortal way without money."

As Aunt Hilda stepped through the door, Salem sprang toward her. "*Please*, take me with you. I promise I won't snitch a nibble! I just want to *sniff* all those tasty treats!"

"Forget it, Salem. You can have a piece for dinner with the rest of us. Bye!" Aunt Hilda waved and closed the door behind her.

Flopping on the floor, Salem covered his face with his paws and sobbed.

"What's wrong with you, Salem?" Sabrina bounced down the stairs. "Are we out of tuna?"

"I certainly hope not!" Salem looked

3

up sharply as Sabrina headed toward the kitchen. His stomach growled and he hurried after her. If he couldn't have fresh fish, canned tuna was the next best thing.

"Speaking of tuna, Sabrina—"

Sabrina poured herself a glass of orange juice, then looked in Salem's dish. "No tuna, Salem. You haven't finished your morning kitty food."

"Pretty Kitty! Yuck." Salem gagged, then leaped onto the counter. "It tastes like cardboard. I may not be a warlock anymore, but I still like the finer things in life. And Icky Kitty isn't one of them."

"But it's full of vitamins." Downing her orange juice, Sabrina smiled. "And it's not fattening."

"I'm not fat!" Annoyed, Salem sucked in his stomach.

"Fat? No. But you are getting a little chubby."

Salem bristled at the insult. "I'm not chubby, either!"

"Yes, you are." Patting Salem's head, Sabrina winked. "Gotta go!"

"Go?" Salem stretched out on the counter. Sabrina was wearing shorts, a T-shirt and sandals. "Where are you going dressed like that?"

"I'm meeting Harvey and Val at the lake. And I'm late." Sabrina pointed at the table. A beach bag, a large towel, a bathing suit, suntan lotion, and a pair of sunglasses appeared.

"Lake?" Salem sat up. "A *real* lake, where frogs and minnows and those little blue and yellow sunfish hang out?"

Grinning, Sabrina zapped up a picnic basket. "I don't know about the min-

nows and sunfish, but all the kids hang out there."

"Sounds like a great place to take your adorable pet cat," Salem hinted. "Your totally *bored* pet cat who *never* gets to go anywhere that's fun."

"Sorry, Salem. The lake's in Westbridge Park and no pets are allowed." Shrugging, Sabrina stuffed her beach things into the bag.

"But—" Salem jumped down. Catching his own fish would be so much *more* exciting than sniffing fish at the market. He rubbed against Sabrina's leg. "You could pretend you don't know me."

Sighing, Sabrina scratched the cat behind his ears. "Can't risk it, Salem. The lifeguards might see you and call Animal Control. Then you'd have to spend the rest of the weekend in the pound."

"But—"

"No way, Salem." Sabrina grabbed her picnic basket and beach bag.

Salem suddenly got a bright idea. He might be able to get into the picnic basket without Sabrina seeing him. Then she wouldn't *know* she was sneaking him into the park.

"See ya, Salem," Sabrina said as she yanked open the back door.

Sooner than you think, Salem thought. The kitchen door swung closed behind Sabrina. He ran toward his cat door.

He jumped back when the big door flew open again.

Sabrina frowned when she saw the surprised cat standing in the open doorway. "Close the door, Salem!"

"I'm a cat. Not a doorman!" Salem huffed.

Sabrina pulled the door closed, but it didn't latch. "What's wrong with this door?"

"The lock must be broken. Guess you'll have to stay home." Salem purred. "We can chase dust motes and unroll the toilet paper in all the bathrooms—"

"You're staying home, Salem. I'm going to the lake," Sabrina said. "I'll just use a spell to keep the door closed."

Salem backed up into the kitchen as Sabrina stood on the porch and pointed.

"Kitchen door with broken lock,
stay closed and solid as a rock."

The door slammed closed and stayed closed.

Salem sighed. Then he heard Aunt Zelda's voice in the living room. Maybe she would give him some tuna.

"I'm leaving now, Dr. Perkins. I'll be there in fifteen minutes."

"Wait!" Salem skidded to a stop as Aunt Zelda hung up the phone. "Could you get me some tuna before you go?"

"Sorry, Salem. I was supposed to be at the Marine Aquarium five minutes ago—"

"Aquarium?" Salem snapped to attention. "Where tasty deep-sea tidbits swim right up to the glass? I'm drooling already!"

"Well, you can stop drooling, Salem,"

9

Aunt Zelda said sternly. "You can't go with me."

"But I love watching fish almost as much as I love eating them!"

Aunt Zelda shook her head. "Dr. Perkins would take away my membership in the Westbridge Science Society if I brought a cat to the aquarium."

"I'll go in disguise!" Salem's golden eyes gleamed with delight.

"Disguised as what?" Aunt Zelda asked.

"Uh—" Salem thought quickly. Aunt Zelda was wearing a black skirt and jacket. "The black fur collar on your jacket! It's brilliant. Dr. Perkins will never know!"

"No. I never wear fur. You can't go and that's final." Aunt Zelda looked back as she walked out the front door.

"Besides, you wouldn't want to be a tasty tidbit for a hungry shark, would you?"

"Sharks don't scare me!"

Aunt Zelda just waved good-bye.

Salem sighed as the door closed. It was going to be another long and boring Saturday afternoon.

11

Chapter 2

Salem wandered into the living room and jumped onto the coffee table. He hated being left alone.

Especially when everyone else was having a good time.

And he had to stay home because he was a cat.

"No pets allowed," Salem muttered. "It's just not fair."

But he was not an ordinary pet. He'd

once been a powerful warlock. But when his attempt to take over the world failed, the Witches' Council sentenced him to one hundred years as a cat. A cat with no magic powers. When he became a warlock again, he *would* take over the world. And his first rule would be that pets could go anywhere.

But that wouldn't help him now.

He was still stuck at home.

With nothing to do.

And the house was way too quiet.

"But I can fix that!" Salem raced to the kitchen. Sabrina's boom box was on the counter. He didn't really like teen music, but the silence was worse.

And even though he wouldn't admit it to anyone else, he *was* getting a bit flabby around the middle.

"A little fanny shaking boom-da-da-

13

boom-boom music is just what the vet ordered. Ten minutes of aerobic dancing will tighten up the old tummy."

Leaping onto the counter, Salem pushed the play button with his paw. Nothing happened. He pushed another button and another. Still nothing happened. He hit the top of the box and the top flipped open. There was a CD inside.

"So why isn't this thing working?"

Stumped, Salem sat back. Then he saw that the boom box wasn't plugged in.

"Rats!" Salem glared at the boom box. Since he couldn't listen to the CD, he thought about playing *with* the CD. Flipping the shiny disk around the kitchen like a Frisbee might be fun—for a few minutes.

But the CD would get scratched.

And that would upset Sabrina.

And there was no one home to take the blame except him.

Sighing, Salem closed the CD player. Then he curled up and closed his eyes. Five seconds later, he opened them again.

He'd already taken three naps this morning, so he wasn't really tired.

What he really wanted was some excitement in his dull life. But that wasn't going to happen today.

Since he couldn't have music or adventure, he decided to settle for a snack. But he wanted fresh fish or tuna, not cat chow. There wasn't any fresh fish in the house. But the cabinet was full of tuna tins.

All he had to do was figure out how to open one.

15

Salem hooked his paw in the cabinet handle and pulled. The door opened easily. He toppled the stack of tuna cans inside. Two cans dropped onto the counter and rolled. He stopped one can with his nose and one with his paw.

"So far so good."

Pleased, Salem pushed one can toward the electric can opener. Putting both front paws around the can, he clamped on tight with his claws. But the can was too heavy to lift.

His stomach rumbled.

Grunting, Salem held on tighter and tried lifting the can again. The can flipped out of his grip and rolled off the edge of the counter. It landed on the floor with a thud.

But it didn't burst open.

"A cat could starve around here!" Furious, Salem batted the second can off the counter. It landed on its side and rolled under the table.

"Tuna, tuna everywhere and not a bite to eat." Depressed, Salem went to his dish. He stared at the few pieces of Pretty Kitty in the bottom of the bowl.

"It's Icky Kitty or nothing, I guess." Salem took a bite and crunched it between his teeth. It still tasted like cardboard. However, when he finished, his stomach stopped growling.

But an endless, boring afternoon stretched before him. Only twenty minutes had passed since Aunt Zelda had left.

Salem groaned as he thought about the schools of colorful fish at the Marine Aquarium.

"Don't think about it," Salem told himself. "You'll drive yourself crazy."

17

As soon as Salem told himself not to think about fish, all he could think about was fish.

Fish swimming behind glass at the aquarium.

Tuna sealed in cans he couldn't open.

The smell of fresh fish on ice at the market. He was sure no one would have noticed a tiny cat bite out of a fin or a tail here and there.

The fish in the park lake that he could be catching with his bare paws . . .

Salem shook his head. He had to do something to take his mind off fish and being bored.

Then he realized there was *one* good thing about being left alone in the house.

No one would yell at him for sharpening his claws on the sofa!

Salem dashed back into the living room. Just as he dug his claws into the couch, he heard a faint chattering.

Salem quickly retracted his claws and looked behind him. No one was there, but he could still hear the noise. He crept across the floor to the den and paused in the doorway.

A squirrel was sitting outside the front window. When it saw Salem, it dropped the acorn it was eating. Fluffing out its tail, the squirrel chattered louder.

Growling, Salem fluffed out his own tail. He wasn't in the mood to be teased. The squirrel lived in the big tree in the front yard, and it liked to taunt him. But whenever he chased it, the squirrel always escaped into the small branches high in the tree.

19

He was a good tree climber, but the squirrel was better.

"And braver," Salem grumbled. Cats could not cling to swaying branches like squirrels.

The squirrel chittered loudly again. It thought it was safe on the other side of the window.

"Wrong!" Crouching, Salem wiggled his haunches. Then he sprang toward the window.

The squirrel leaped to the ground. Then it realized the cat couldn't get out and turned to stare.

Salem glared back through the window. Chasing the squirrel would be almost as much fun as fishing. But the squirrel would be gone before he could get out of the house through his cat door in the kitchen.

20

The squirrel sat up on its haunches and chittered softly. It was laughing at him.

Salem pressed his nose against the window. He gasped when the window moved! It was the kind that opened out like his cat door. And it wasn't latched!

"But I'll have the last laugh today."

Tensing, Salem gathered all his energy. Then he pushed the window open and jumped through.

The surprised squirrel blinked, then took off across the yard.

Salem ran after it. "Wahoo!"

The chase was on!

Chapter 3

Salem ran as fast as he could, but he couldn't catch the squirrel. It darted up the trunk of the big tree and stopped on the first large branch.

Out of breath, Salem sat down at the base of the tall oak. He was too winded to climb. Besides, he couldn't follow the squirrel into the high branches.

When he looked up, the squirrel chittered and flicked its bushy tail.

Salem growled. He didn't like being laughed at by a smug squirrel that could outrun him. He hadn't even gotten close to the speedy critter during the mad dash across the yard.

Frowning, Salem touched his stomach. He *was* getting fat.

Bonk!

An acorn bounced off Salem's head. "Ow!"

The insult was more than Salem could stand. Hissing, he leaped onto the tree trunk and began to climb.

The squirrel ran to the end of the branch.

"Don't look down," Salem warned himself when he reached the large branch. He kept his eyes on the squirrel as he carefully crept out on the limb.

The squirrel calmly munched an acorn.

23

When Salem was halfway across, the squirrel jumped onto a leafy branch dangling from above. The movement made the end of the big branch bounce slightly.

"Oh, no!" Salem shrieked. "I'm gonna fall!"

Clamping his claws onto the branch, Salem hung on. He heard the squirrel laughing at him from its higher perch, but he didn't care anymore. He just wanted to get back on solid ground.

Without falling.

Salem was not a clumsy cat. But every now and then he fell off something because he slipped or got distracted. He *always* landed on his feet.

But there was a first time for everything.

Sooner or later he wouldn't land on his feet.

24

And he didn't want his luck to run out when he fell out of a tree!

Then he wouldn't be a fat cat. He'd be a flat cat.

Taking a deep breath, Salem slowly began to back up. His toes hurt from gripping so hard, but he didn't dare relax. He didn't even flinch when the squirrel dropped another acorn that just missed him.

When his back end hit the trunk, Salem sighed with relief. He quickly scrambled down the trunk to the ground.

High in the tree, the squirrel chattered, but Salem didn't look up. His feline dignity had suffered enough damage. After giving his sleek, black fur a few casual licks to hide his embarrassment, he slowly walked away.

Salem kept walking until he rounded the corner of the house and was out of sight from the squirrel. Then he raced toward his cat door.

The cat chow had tasted awful, but it had satisfied his hunger. Chasing the squirrel had been fun, even if the nasty little beast had gotten away again. That had satisfied his hunger for adventure. Now he was ready for a nap.

Nap number four for the day, if I'm not mistaken, he thought.

Anxious to curl up on the sofa, Salem charged the small opening in the back door. He expected the plastic flap to flip up when he ran through. Instead, he hit a solid barrier.

Thunk!

"Ooof!" Dazed, Salem staggered backward. Shaking his head, he stared at the plastic flap. He could see through it. But when he pushed on it, the plastic didn't budge.

Then he remembered Sabrina's spell.

"Kitchen door with broken lock,
stay closed and solid as a rock."

When Sabrina had used magic to keep the big door closed, she had made the cat door solid as a rock, too!

"This can't be happening!" Panicking, Salem scratched at the hard, plastic flap. "Let me in!"

No one was home to hear him.

And the flap was firmly locked in place by Sabrina's magic. It wouldn't open until she removed the spell.

But Sabrina wouldn't be home for hours!

27

"I'll starve by sunset," Salem moaned. *How did I get stuck out here?*

Then he remembered that the front window was open. It was a high jump from the ground, but at least he could get back inside.

Salem relaxed as he strolled to the front of the house. He had been so intent on catching the squirrel, he hadn't noticed that it was a beautiful day.

The noon sun warmed his back. He arched his back. Wisps of cloud dotted the blue sky like fluffy, white sailing ships. He thought about chasing one. A slight, cooling breeze ruffled his fur. He stopped to stretch. Colorful flowers grew in clumps around the front porch and along the walk. *I wouldn't be a cat if I* didn't *stop to smell them.* Busy bees buzzed around the bright blooms, gathering nectar for honey and encouraging the cat to keep moving.

Salem paused under the window. He spent two seconds wondering where the squirrel had gone. Maybe after his nap he'd come back outside. If he hid and waited patiently, he could take the squirrel by surprise. Of course, he'd never actually attack the squirrel, but he'd give it a good scare. Then he'd be the one laughing!

Yawning, Salem arched his back again to loosen up. Then he took a deep breath, crouched, and sprang.

Thunk!

"Ow!"

The window was closed!

"Who declared this 'bonk the cat on the head' day?"

Stunned, Salem dug his claws into the

ledge so he wouldn't fall. The window must've closed after he came through it before. *No matter*, he thought. *It's unlocked.* Clinging to the narrow wooden frame, he carefully lifted one paw. He batted the window to make it swing open. It didn't move.

Craning his neck, Salem looked through the glass and gasped. The latch had fallen into place when the window had slammed closed.

It was locked.

"Nooo! It can't be!" Salem beat on the glass. All he got for his effort was a bruised paw.

The window didn't open.

Salem couldn't believe it. He really was locked out of the house!

"Now what am I going to do?"

Salem jumped back to the ground

and breathed deeply to calm himself. Then he tried to convince himself that things could be worse.

He couldn't get into the house, but it wasn't raining.

The squirrel wasn't hanging around making fun of him, either.

He had just eaten, so he wasn't hungry.

Well, he was still a cat, so, in a way, he was always hungry.

Feeling foolish for being afraid, Salem stretched out on the lush, green grass. The sun was warm and soothing. First he'd take a nice, long nap. Then he'd go exploring.

Yawning, Salem closed his eyes. There wasn't anything in his own front yard that could hurt him—

Grrrr!

Salem's eyes snapped open. *Was that my stomach?*

Something growled again.

The deep, throaty snarl made two very important facts perfectly clear to Salem.

It was a very *big* dog, and it was very, very *close*.

"I'm doomed!" Salem wailed.

Chapter 4

If I'm going down, I'm going down fighting!"

Salem jumped to his feet. The fur on his back and tail stood up. He bared his fangs and hissed. Acting tough was a cat's only defense against a big dog.

That, and hiding in a very tiny place.

But he didn't see a dog.

"Rufff! Arf, arf, arf!"

The sound of frantic barking chilled

Salem to the bone. He didn't see the dog because—

"It's behind me!" Salem leaped straight up and twisted his body in mid-air. Spitting and hissing, he landed facing in the opposite direction.

No dog.

Salem blinked. Maybe he was so upset about being locked outside, he was hearing things.

"Great. Now I'm going bonkers."

"Woof! Arf, arf!"

Nope.

There was a dog all right.

But Salem wasn't in any danger of being attacked by the crazed canine.

The German shepherd was barking from the fenced-in backyard next door. A new family had just moved into the house.

With a sigh of relief, Salem sat down. The dog was big, but it didn't look full-grown yet. *Just a puppy! No problem.*

The German shepherd stopped barking and glared at him through a space between the fence boards.

When Salem stretched, the dog began yapping and scratching at the fence again.

"Chill, Bozo!"

Startled, the dog shut up and backed off a step. Obviously, it was surprised to hear a cat talk like a human.

Salem chuckled softly. This was the chance of a lifetime!

There was no way the dog could dig under or jump over the fence. He was perfectly safe. He couldn't pass up an opportunity to taunt the dog just like the annoying squirrel taunted him. Es-

pecially since the canine had scared him out of two of his nine lives.

Crouching, Salem fixed the dog with a steady gaze and slowly moved forward.

The dog whimpered and poked its nose through the pickets.

Suddenly, Salem charged the fence. "Yee-hah!"

The dog yelped and jumped back as Salem skidded to a halt inches from the fence.

"What kind of chicken-hearted dog are you?" Salem asked in a mocking tone. "Afraid of a little kitty cat?"

Barking furiously, the dog sprang toward the fence.

Salem sat down just beyond reach.

The dog began to dig under the boards. Tufts of grass and dirt flew in all directions.

"Hey, Bozo with the long snout!" Salem chuckled. "You think you're pretty tough, don't you?"

The dog snapped and snarled.

"I'm soooo impressed." Salem yawned.

"Champ!" A young boy's voice called. "What's the matter, boy?"

"Champ?" Salem muttered. "I like Bozo better."

Easing back from the fence, Salem pretended to groom himself as he listened and watched.

The boy looked to be about nine years old. He scratched Champ behind the ears when the dog romped over. "Dad's gonna have a fit if you don't stop digging up the lawn."

Panting, Champ wiggled his hindquarters.

Salem rolled his eyes. Dogs had no sense of dignity when it came to humans. No *cat* would ever put on such a disgusting display of emotion just because it was happy to see its people. Cats pretended they didn't care.

"What *is* his problem, Jonathan?" A younger girl came out of the garage side door. She stood on tiptoe to look over the gate into her backyard.

"I don't know, Kathy." Worried, Jonathan frowned. "Maybe he's upset about moving to a new place."

"Or maybe Champ doesn't like that cat." Kathy pointed at Salem.

Who, me? Salem blinked, trying to look innocent. He couldn't talk out loud in front of mortals. It was okay to freak out a dumb dog. But he'd be in big trouble with Aunt Hilda and Aunt

Zelda if he did *anything* to make the new neighbors suspect they were witches.

He was pretty sure they wouldn't be happy if the neighbors complained about their pet cat harassing Champ, either. The German shepherd wouldn't get into trouble. *Nooooo, everyone expected dogs to harass cats.*

"Shoo!" Jonathan yelled. "Go away, you pesky cat!"

"Yeow!" Salem ducked as a clump of grassy dirt sailed by him. Surprised, he hissed. He was in his own yard, minding his own business. Besides, the dog had started it!

"Hey!" Kathy snapped. "Don't do that, Jonathan. It's not his fault he's a cat and Champ hates cats."

Yeah! Realizing Kathy was a friend,

39

Salem decided to make the most of it. Faking a limp, he hobbled over and rubbed against her leg.

"Are you hurt, kitty?" Kathy patted Salem's head, then shot an angry glance at her brother. "See what you did? He's limping!"

Heh heh heh. Take that, Jonathan!

"That dirt clod didn't hit him, Kathy! I just wanted to scare him off." Picking up a stick, Jonathan threw it across his backyard.

Champ ran after it.

Salem sighed. He loved batting crumpled papers and catnip mice around the house. But he rarely played when humans were watching.

Not unless his playing disrupted what they were doing.

Like shredding the paper when Aunt

Hilda and Aunt Zelda were wrapping birthday presents.

Or rolling Christmas ornaments under the couch when they tried decorating trees the mortal way.

Dogs obviously didn't have that much self-control.

Shaking her head, Kathy squatted down. "You really shouldn't get too close to Champ, kitty. He doesn't like cats much at all."

Champ doesn't scare me!

Salem shoved his head under the girl's hand. He purred as she rubbed the itchy spot on his neck.

"Jonathan! Kathy!" A woman called. "Time to go grocery shopping!"

"I've got to go, kitty. Bye." Giving Salem a final pat, Kathy ran back into the garage.

"Hurry up, Jonathan!" A man shouted.

"Coming, Dad!"

Salem moved back several feet as a station wagon pulled out of the garage. Jonathan ran through the gate and hopped into the back seat with his sister.

As the car roared down the street, Salem ambled back toward the front porch. Meeting Champ and the two kids had been entertaining. He'd teased the dog and gotten a nice rub from the girl. Now all he wanted to do was stretch out on the porch railing for a nice, long snooze in the sun.

Champ started barking again.

Salem didn't walk faster or look back. The sound wore on his nerves, but he didn't want the dog to think he really *was* afraid.

"Trying to sleep with all that noise might be hard, though."

Then Champ suddenly stopped barking.

Alarmed, Salem stopped. He slowly turned his head to look back.

Uh-oh!

Jonathan hadn't latched the gate!

The shepherd bolted through the opening and charged straight for him.

Chapter 5

Salem was running for his life within a split second.

Champ quickly closed the gap between them.

"This is no time to finish second!"

But Salem knew he wouldn't reach safety in time. The porch and the tall oak where the squirrel lived were too far away. The dog would catch him before he got there.

That thought gave Salem a burst of energy. Running faster, he headed for a smaller tree by the front corner of the house. It was closer than the porch and the tall oak. He might just make it.

Champ barked wildly as he gained ground.

And Salem was slowing down.

"Just a few more feet—"

Gathering his last bit of strength, Salem leaped onto the tree trunk. His claws were already out. He latched onto the bark just as the big puppy reached the tree.

Salem scrambled upward an instant before the dog's jaws clamped onto his tail.

When he reached the first branch, Salem paused to look down. He was out of breath and his tired legs trembled.

45

The angry, barking dog jumped.

Terrified, Salem stared at the dog's sharp teeth. Champ got so close, he could feel the canine's hot breath on his nose. He had to go higher.

Digging in, Salem slowly climbed to the next branch.

Below him, Champ continued to snarl and leap. But the dog couldn't jump high enough to reach him.

Exhausted, Salem collapsed on his stomach. He braced his back end against the trunk. His legs dangled on both sides of the branch. The tree wasn't the best place to take a nap, but he was too tired to be choosy.

Resting his chin on the rough bark, Salem closed his eyes.

Then felt himself slip to one side!
Whoa!

Instinctively, Salem clamped his claws onto the branch.

He wouldn't just be a flat cat if he fell off.

He'd be Champ chow!

"Not exactly a pleasant thought." Easing back onto the branch, Salem looked down again.

Champ was lying on the ground, staring up at him. The dog's lip curled back in a snarl. Then he yawned, lowered his head and closed his eyes.

Salem sighed.

Being locked out of the house was bad. Being trapped in a tree by a huge dog was worse. Now he couldn't even take a nap!

At least the dog hadn't caught him.

And now that Champ had dozed off, he wasn't barking or growling, either.

As long as Salem could hang on and stay awake, he'd be safe until Sabrina or her aunts got home.

"No problem. I'll just—"

Bonk!

"Ouch!" Salem flinched as an acorn bounced off his back.

Bonk, bonk! Bonk!

Three more acorns fell. One hit his head and two hit the branch.

Salem looked up.

The squirrel was back! It chattered with amused delight in the branches high above Salem's perch. Then it dropped another acorn.

Bonk!

The nut hit Salem on the nose.

"Ow!"

A sparrow landed on a branch two feet in front of Salem, just beyond his grasp. It blinked its beady eyes, then whistled merrily when another acorn fell.

The acorn hit the branch between Salem's front paws. Then it bounced up and smacked him in the chin.

"That does it!"

Salem could accept being beaten by a dog that was bigger and faster than he was.

But he would *not* just lie there and let the rotten, little squirrel drop acorns on him all afternoon!

Especially with a bird as a witness.

Salem's reputation as the fierce master of the yard would be ruined! He'd never live down the humiliation.

"I'm a cat! I have my pride!"

Rising on unsteady legs, Salem lunged at the sparrow and swatted with his paw.

49

The bird flew away unharmed.

Salem belly flopped onto the branch.

"I meant to do that," Salem said. Like all cats, he would never admit that he missed.

The squirrel chittered. It was enjoying the cat's embarrassing position.

Champ snored.

After being locked out, laughed at, chased, trapped, and acorn bombed, Salem couldn't take another blow to his feline pride.

"This is all your fault!" Salem shouted at the squirrel. "And you're gonna pay!"

Turning on wobbly legs, Salem crept back along the branch to the tree trunk. Watching the squirrel, he began to climb.

The squirrel waited until the cat was

four feet away. Then it dashed higher and ran out on a smaller branch. The branch swayed and bent under its weight.

Salem was sure he had the squirrel trapped. Then he realized that the branches of the small oak mingled with the branches of the large oak.

The squirrel leaped into the leafy canopy of the bigger oak tree.

There was no way Salem could follow. He was too heavy.

But the squirrel's method of escape gave Salem an inspired idea.

Salem leaned against the trunk to study his surroundings. He was halfway up the smaller tree. The branches here weren't as thick as the lower ones. However, the end of the nearest branch extended over the porch roof by two feet!

He could use the branch as a bridge to the top of the porch!

"If that squirrel can do it, so can I!"

Salem sharpened his claws on the bark. One slip and he would fall. Landing on his feet wouldn't help him if Champ woke up.

Taking a deep breath, Salem gripped the branch and started inching toward the end. When he was halfway across, the limb began to bend.

Salem gritted his teeth and kept going. But the farther out he moved, the more the branch bent. It was too late to turn back when he realized he had made a big mistake.

The end of the branch didn't reach over the porch roof when it bent. It dipped toward the ground.

Salem hooked his claws in the leafy

twigs at the end of the branch. He squeezed his eyes shut as the limb sagged farther down.

"Look out below!"

But he didn't crash into the dirt.

Surprised, Salem opened his eyes.

He was swinging two feet off the ground.

And Champ was glaring at him nose to nose!

Chapter 6

Oops."

Clinging to the branch, Salem dipped and swayed in front of the dog.

Like bait on a fishing pole!

Champ bared his teeth.

"I'm not gonna be chomped by Champ!"

Salem did the only thing a cat could do. He smacked the dog in the snout with his claws.

The dog yelped and jumped backward.

Salem didn't hesitate. Dropping to the ground, he ran toward the porch. With luck and a tucked-in tummy, he could squeeze through the slats around the base of the porch.

Champ was definitely too big to follow him under there.

"If I can get there ahead of him!"

"Ruff! Arf, arf, arf!"

Champ was coming up behind him fast.

"Yeow!" Salem screeched as the dog's teeth closed on the furred tip of his tail!

Putting on a burst of speed, Salem swerved to the right. His tail slipped through the slobbering puppy's teeth.

The dog stopped to spit the fur out of his mouth.

And Salem realized that he had made another big mistake.

He was running across the open yard *away* from the house. There was nowhere to hide!

Champ circled around him.

Salem put on the brakes as the dog turned and bounded toward him. Spinning around, he ran back toward the porch.

Barking, Champ raced around him again.

Salem slid to a halt as the dog whirled to face him. But Champ didn't charge. The dog had him cornered and seemed to be toying with him, which was curious.

"Like a cat playing with a mouse."

Either Champ was using cat tactics . . .

Or the sting of sharp cat claws on his nose had made the dog more cautious.

Salem eyed the dog warily. His tired legs felt like wet noodles. But the game wasn't over yet.

No dog was as cunning as a cat.

Besides, dogs didn't have the patience to tease their prey before making their final move.

Salem was not a foolish cat. He knew that Champ hadn't given up. The dog just didn't want another painful swat from his claws.

But sooner or later Champ would give in to his canine instincts and start chasing him again.

Salem had to escape *now*.

A desperate cat could outwit a cautious dog.

"You may be faster and bigger than me, Champ. But you're not smarter!"

When Champ lowered his head to

charge, Salem fluffed out his fur, bared his fangs, and hissed.

The puppy hesitated.

Arching his back, Salem flattened his ears against his head. That made him look more menacing. Then he took two slow steps to the side.

Growling, Champ slowly moved a few steps in the opposite direction.

Salem sidestepped again.

The dog matched the movement, going the other way.

Then Salem did something Champ didn't expect. Spitting and hissing, he charged toward the dog.

Startled, Champ backed off a few feet.

That was exactly what Salem had been hoping for. The dog was no longer blocking his path to the porch. The cat took off like a shot.

Champ immediately took off after him, but he wasn't quite fast enough.

Salem reached the porch several strides ahead of the dog and dove through the space between the slats.

And got stuck!

The boards pressed against Salem's pudgy sides, holding him firmly in place.

"A fine time to find out I really am a fat cat!"

Wiggling didn't help. Forcing himself to stop struggling, Salem sucked in his stomach and lunged. He tumbled into the dark space under the porch just as Champ ran into the boards.

"Safe!"

Panting, Salem lay down on the cool ground in the middle of the space. He didn't bother to shake off the bits of

dirt, dry grass, and cobwebs that clung to his fur. He was so tired, he couldn't move. Fortunately, he didn't have to.

Champ couldn't even get his squashed snout through the space between the boards.

"Give it up, Champ," Salem said wearily.

The dog cocked his head, listening.

Salem decided to try reasoning with him. "You can't reach me in here. Fun's over. So why don't you just go home?"

Champ growled.

Salem wasn't thrilled about being trapped under the porch. It was dark and dirty, and the ground was damp. With luck, Sabrina or one of her aunts would come home sooner than he expected.

Or the new neighbors would return. When they found out Champ was missing, they'd catch him and lock him back in his yard where he belonged.

"At least, I'm safe under here. I'd rather be dirty and damp than kitty treat for a dog." Salem shuddered at the thought.

Champ rammed the slats with his head.

Salem flinched. If Champ broke the boards, he was done for!

"Just how many of my nine cat lives do I have left?" Salem blinked, then decided he really didn't want to know.

"All you're going to get doing that is a big headache, Champ!"

Being a dog and not nearly as smart as a cat, Champ hit the boards half a dozen times before he gave up.

"It's over, Champ!" Salem yelled. "Scram!"

Champ started digging.

"Uh-oh." Salem groaned. Even though he was in danger, he admired the dog's determination. "It's gonna be a real short time out."

The soft garden ground around the porch was easy digging. Brown dirt, green leaves, and colorful flower petals flew under Champ's paws. The dog would be under the porch in five minutes—or less!

"First thing to remember," Salem said. "Don't panic. Think!"

He couldn't escape on the house side. The foundation wall was made of solid cinder blocks and cement.

Salem studied the slats on the other two sides. The boards were all spaced the same distance apart—except for one at the far corner. That space looked to be just a little bit wider.

"I just hope it's *enough* wider." Salem sighed. As much as he hated the idea, he had to go on a diet. "If I live through the afternoon."

Champ tested his hole. It was big enough for his head. He kept digging.

Saving his energy, Salem crouched and waited.

He had a plan.

But success depended on perfect timing.

And whether he had the strength to run at top speed one more time.

Chapter 7

While Champ dug, Salem slowly backed into the front corner. He stuck his tail through the space between the slat and the corner post.

"Come and get me, Champ."

"Rufff."

Crouching, Salem kept his gaze on the dog and inched backward. He pushed his hindquarters through the space and stopped when he was half in and half out.

Champ was too busy digging to notice.

When Champ stuck his front legs under the slats, Salem tensed.

"Not yet. Wait—"

Champ wasn't real bright, but he wasn't totally stupid, either. For a dog. Salem didn't dare make his move too soon.

Grunting, the dog shoved his head and his shoulders under the slats.

Salem's heart beat wildly. The slat and the post pressed against his chubby sides. He didn't think he'd get stuck again, but he wasn't sure. Every nerve was on edge as the dog slowly crawled into the space under the porch.

Dogs were very predictable. Part of

Salem's escape plan depended on the shepherd acting like every other dog he had ever met.

"Ready, set . . ."

The instant Champ's back legs cleared the hole, Salem pushed himself backward.

"I'm out of here!"

Salem's fat tummy became wedged in the space.

"Or not!" Frantic, Salem dug in with his front claws.

Fortunately, Champ was too big to stand up under the low porch. Crouching, the dog awkwardly lunged toward the trapped cat.

Bits of fur flew as Salem heaved himself backward. He popped out of the space just as the dog shoved his flat snout through it.

"Woof! Arf, arf, arf!" Furious, the dog began digging in the corner, now trying to get *out* from under the porch.

Salem took off running toward the new neighbors' house. He didn't look back because it would slow him down.

He knew what the dog's next move would be.

Champ would stop digging in the corner and squeeze out of his first hole.

Right about now.

Salem's keen cat ears heard the sound of grunting and scraping.

Yep.

Salem raced for the fence. Within a few seconds Champ would be out from under the porch and chasing him again.

"Ruff! Ruff, arf, arf!"

Bingo!

As Salem ran past the tall oak tree, he heard the squirrel chattering angrily above him.

"Bet *he* can't wait to see me get done in by a dog."

Being a cat and curious, Salem looked up. He faltered in surprise.

The squirrel wasn't screaming at him! Tail fluffed and nose twitching, the little beast was yelling at Champ!

But Salem had lost precious ground checking out the squirrel.

"Curiosity isn't gonna kill this cat!"

Forcing his tired legs to move faster, Salem ran on. He skidded as he turned to enter the open gate. From the corner of his eye, he saw the squirrel drop an acorn.

On Champ!

Bonk!

Startled, the dog hesitated when the acorn hit him on the head.

Amazed, Salem bolted through the gate. The squirrel was on *his* side! It had slowed down the dog, buying him time to increase his lead again.

He couldn't stop to wonder why.

His life depended on speed.

And on Champ being too dumb to realize what he was doing.

Salem ran toward the far corner of Champ's backyard.

Barking, the dog ran through the gate and charged after him.

Salem circled back along the rear section of fence.

Champ could easily have cut him off. But Champ didn't think of that. He was a dog and dogs loved to *chase*.

"Which is a good thing for me!"

Salem barreled back toward the gate along the side fence with Champ gaining fast.

"I'm gonna make it. I'm gonna make it."

Heart pounding and lungs bursting, Salem zoomed toward the opening in the fence. When he was through the gate, he whirled and dashed behind it.

"Almost home free!"

Panting and shaking, Salem leaned against the wooden gate. After he pushed it closed, Champ would be safely locked in his backyard again.

Except that the bottom of the gate was stuck against the ground.

It wouldn't move!

Chapter 8

Time was running out!

Champ was only a few feet away.

Backing up a step, Salem threw himself against the stubborn gate!

"Oof!"

Salem bounced off the wooden boards and sprawled on the ground. Exhausted and breathless, he didn't have the energy to get up.

The gate hinges squeaked.

Champ charged toward the opening. "Ruff! Arf, arf!"

The gate seemed to swing closed in slow motion.

"Come on! Close!"

The gate slammed shut.

Thwap!

The metal latch fell into place.

Clunk.

And Champ ran into the barrier.

Thunk!

"Ouch much!" Salem watched the dog through a crack between the boards. He'd lured the dog back into his own yard and circled back to shut the gate.

Dazed, Champ shook his head. Then he pressed his nose against the gate and stared at the cat, making those dog whimpering noises.

"What a loser!" Salem chuckled.

Snorting, Champ dropped down on his stomach. Resting his chin on his front paws, he closed his eyes.

"That's it?" Salem asked, annoyed. "I win and you're just gonna go to sleep?"

Champ yawned, but he didn't open his eyes.

"You ruined my day, Champ!" Salem shouted. "And almost turned me into canine lunch munchies! Aren't you just a *little* upset that I got away?"

Champ snored.

"Guess not." Salem huffed as he dragged himself to his feet. "Dogs have *no* pride."

Cats, however, had plenty.

Salem was exhausted, and every muscle in his body ached. Even so, he

raised his tail and held his head high as he walked home.

He had won!

Against the odds!

Against a bigger and faster foe.

"It's great to be a cat!" Salem paused. "Until I can be a warlock again, anyway. I should probably be glad Drell didn't turn me into a *dog* for a hundred years!"

Feeling wonderful in spite of his aches and pains, Salem crawled up the porch steps. Curling up in the sun, he scanned the tall oak. He didn't see the squirrel.

Yawning, Salem closed his eyes. He fell asleep instantly and dreamed that Sabrina was calling him.

"Salem! What are you doing out here?"

Salem's eyes popped open. It wasn't

a dream. Sabrina was standing on the walk, staring at him.

"You locked my cat door with your spell!"

"I did?" Sabrina winced. "I'm sorry, Salem. How did you get outside then?"

"I jumped through the front window, but it locked when it slammed and I couldn't get *back* inside after the squirrel *bonked* me with acorns!"

"Bonked you?" Sabrina laughed. "That cute, little gray squirrel that lives in the oak?"

"He's weird, but he's not cute," Salem muttered as he stretched, then groaned. He was stiff and sore all over.

"Well, if you're tired of lazing around in the sun—"

"Tired? I'm totally pooped!" Salem sputtered indignantly. "But I haven't been lazing around in the sun. I spent most of the afternoon trying *not* to get chomped by the dog that just moved in next door!"

Sabrina looked toward the new neighbors' house. "I don't see a dog."

"Of course not! Champ went to sleep after I tricked him back into his fenced yard. I barely escaped with my life!"

"Sounds like you've had an exciting day."

"Too exciting." Calming down, Salem sighed. "Why are you home so early?"

Sabrina shrugged. "I felt so bad about leaving you home by yourself, I came back to get you."

"You did?" Salem perked his ears

forward. *Ouch!* Even they hurt! "What about the rule against letting pets into the park?"

"I'm a witch! I decided that if a lifeguard saw you, I could just point you into Harvey's car or something." Sabrina smiled. "Ready? The lake is full of fish that are so waiting to be caught."

Salem moaned. Two hours ago he would have jumped at the chance. He loved catching fish with his bare paws. Now, he hardly had enough strength to twitch a whisker.

"Actually, I'd be tickled pink if you'd just *point* me onto the sofa." Salem yawned. "I really need a nap."

"You got it." Sabrina raised her finger. "One pink catnap coming up!"

Pink!

"No!" Salem shook his head, knowing Sabrina was still getting the hang of being a witch. "I didn't mean *pink*—"

Sabrina's magic finger flicked and Salem was suddenly sitting on the soft sofa cushions.

He shut his eyes. After his awful afternoon, being turned into a pink cat would be too much.

Opening one eye, Salem slowly looked down. His fur was still black.

Relieved, Salem turned around in circles until he found exactly the right spot. Then he collapsed. With a contented sigh, he closed his eyes.

Nap number four? Or was it five . . .

Salem drifted off thinking about Aunt Hilda's promise of fresh fish for dinner.

Clink.

Salem slowly opened one eye.

Clink. Clunk, clink.

"Now what?"

Glancing at the front window, Salem saw the squirrel looking in. It hit the window with its front paw.

Clink.

"What do you want?"

The squirrel chattered.

Salem wondered. Why *had* the squirrel tried to save him from the dog?

Because it liked him?

Because it liked *taunting* him?

Or maybe because it just didn't like crazed dogs running loose in its yard.

"Our yard." Salem corrected himself.

Either way, the little beast obviously wanted him to come out and play.

Ignoring the squirrel, Salem closed

his eyes again. He was too tired to do anything but sleep.

Besides, he hadn't enjoyed being chased around the yard by Champ all afternoon. Now that he knew what it felt like, chasing the squirrel didn't seem like quite so much fun.

"At least, not today." Salem purred. "But just wait until tomorrow!"

Cat Care Tips

#1 Never leave the door to the clothes dryer open. Some cats like to sleep in the dryer and can get hurt if the dryer is turned on.

#2 Never give your cat any medication without checking with your veterinarian. Things such as aspirin and Tylenol can make cats very sick.

#3 If you buy medication such as flea products at the pet store or grocery store, make sure that the label says it is okay to give it to cats. Follow the directions carefully. It is best to use only products that your veterinarian has given you, and never give your cat medication that was meant for a dog.

—Laura E. Smiley, MS, DVM, Dipl. ACVIM
Gwynedd Veterinary Hospital

Meet up with suspense and mystery in

THE CLUES BROTHERS™

#1 The Gross Ghost Mystery
#2 The Karate Clue
#3 First Day, Worst Day
#4 Jump Shot Detectives
#5 Dinosaur Disaster
#6 WHo Took the Book?
#7 The Abracadabra Case
#8 The Doggone Dectectives
#9 The Pumped-Up Pizza Problem
#10 The Walking Snowman
#11 The Monster in the Lake

By Franklin W. Dixon

Look for a brand-new story every other month
at your local bookseller

A MINSTREL BOOK

Published by Pocket Books

1398-06

**Do your younger brothers and sisters
want to read books like yours?**

Let them know there are books just for them!

THE NANCY DREW NOTEBOOKS ®

Look for a brand-new story every other month

Available from Minstrel® Books
Published by Pocket Books

1356-02